Wallace & Gromit
THE CURSE OF THE WERE-RABBIT
Novelization

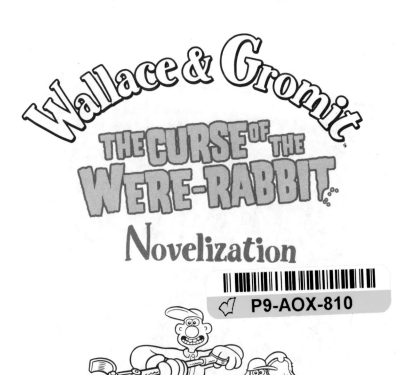

P9-AOX-810

Adapted from the screenplay by Penny Worms
Screenplay by Mark Burton, Bob Baker,
Steve Box, and Nick Park

PSS!
PRICE STERN SLOAN

Chapter One

It was a dark and misty night. A full moon cast eerie shadows around PC Mackintosh as he strolled through the dark streets of a small English town on his midnight beat. All was well. Or so he thought.

PC Mackintosh paused to read the poster in a corner-shop window:

GIANT VEGETABLE
COMPETITION—
TOTTINGTON HALL

Only five days' propagation to go!

"Vegetable mad, this lot!" he muttered as a huge shadow loomed over his shoulder on to the poster. With lightning reflexes, he grabbed his truncheon and spun around. His heart was pounding; fear seeped quickly into his bones. Scanning the road, he saw the source of the shadow—scuttling across a street lamp was a large moth. It was magnified to monstrous proportions by the light from the lamp, but it was actually no bigger than the policeman's thumb.

Feeling a little foolish, he shook his head. "Albert Mackintosh," he said to himself, "you need an 'oliday. Too many late shifts—that's what it is." He checked his watch and, rather relieved that his shift was over, he headed for home.

But if PC Mackintosh had been as sharp as he used to be as a young police constable, he might have sensed that all was not well.

Something was lurking in the shadows—and it was *no moth*. As soon as the coast was clear, it moved toward a nearby garden and slowly pushed open the gate. It moved silently down the path to the giant vegetable patch, passing a garden gnome on its way. The gnome's head turned as it passed. Then the gnome's eyes started to flash.

A second later, in another part of town, lights started flashing in the eyes of an old lady. She was seated, silent and still, looking out of the window as if she were part of the furniture. In fact, she *was* part of the furniture: Mrs. Mulch's portrait had been hanging in the dining room of Wallace and Gromit's house ever since she became one of their most valued clients. Inventor Wallace and his faithful pooch Gromit had made quite a success of their new business together: Anti-pesto Ltd. Humane Pest Control. They had been hired to protect the townsfolks' vegetables in the lead-up to the Giant

Vegetable Competition. The flashing-eyes signal was advance warning that something was wrong in Mrs. Mulch's vegetable garden. Something was very wrong.

In the kitchen, a kettle started to boil. The steam from it turned the sails of a small windmill, making a steel rod jiggle up and down. The vibrations traveled up the rod, through the floorboards to a metal hand under Gromit's bed. A finger on the hand prodded the bed vigorously. Gromit woke up with a start and prepared for what was coming next . . . Quick as a flash, his bed tipped up and Gromit disappeared through a hole in the wall.

In Wallace's bedroom a hatch opened beside his bed and a waiter's hand appeared. It was holding a plate, on which was Wallace's favorite delicacy—a large chunk of cheese. The hand wafted the cheese under Wallace's nose. Being so deliciously sensitive to the smell of cheese, Wallace's

nose moved toward the wonderful aroma—
then BAM! The hatch slammed in his face
and he was tipped through the wall. Now,
Wallace too was awake and falling . . .

"Whoaaaaaa!" Wallace cried as he slid
down a chute and was reunited with his old
buddy Gromit. In the blink of an eye, a set
of fantastic automated inventions dressed
them in hats, boots, and jumpsuits, pausing
only to pour them a nice mug of tea before
hydraulically firing them into their waiting
van.

Anti-pesto Ltd. was ready to go.

Without delay, the van was cranked into
action and they were off, speeding toward
Mrs. Mulch's garden.

Like a police SWAT team, Wallace and
Gromit rolled out of the van and took up their
positions on either side of the garden gate.
Wallace peeped through a hole in the fence
just in time to see a shadowy shape pass by.
What could it be? A vegetable-gobbling

beastie? Wallace signaled to Gromit to get ready with a large sack. Then he catapulted his faithful companion into the garden. Gromit brought the sack down over the beast.

"Cracking job, Gromit!" Wallace said as the bagged creature struggled furiously to get out.

Lights began to go on down the street.

Mr. Dibber looked out of his window at the mayhem in Mrs. Mulch's garden. "What's going on?" he called.

Gromit was being dragged around the garden by what looked like a sack with legs.

Wallace grabbed the beast. "Gotcha!" he cried, with obvious relief. "Thieving little monster."

Gromit whipped off the sack to reveal the terrible intruder. Except it wasn't a monster at all—it was a cute little rabbit hanging on with all his might to a giant pumpkin that he was hoping might be his supper for the night.

"Oooh, me prize pumpkin!" exclaimed Mrs. Mulch, appearing with Mr. Mulch at their back door. "Me pride and joy! You've saved it, Anti-pesto!"

"All in a night's work, Mrs. Mulch," replied Wallace, lifting up the tiny intruder. "Left to his own devices, this is the ultimate vegetable-destroying machine!" He turned to Gromit. "Prepare detainment chamber, Gromit!"

They plonked the rabbit into a cage at the back of the van to great applause from the pajama-clad neighbors.

"Bless you, Anti-pesto!" said the vicar in his nightgown. "With you out there protecting our veggies, the most important event of the year is safe!"

Chapter Two

The following morning, Gromit was in the kitchen preparing breakfast. He chopped a mountain of carrots and poured them down a chute to a cage full of hungry bunnies. Then he pulled the Get-U-Up lever to get Wallace out of bed. Wallace slid out from between his sheets and down the Get-U-Up chute.

"Ooof!" He was firmly wedged in the Get-U-Up trapdoor leading to the dining room. "Gromit, old pal. Happened again! I'll need assistance!"

Gromit tutted and pulled the Assistance

lever. A huge mallet bashed Wallace through the trapdoor and into his breakfast chair, like a fat peg through a thin hole.

"I'm sure that hole's getting smaller," he said.

Gromit raised an eyebrow—Wallace needed to slim down or he'd have to make that trapdoor bigger. Gromit placed the morning papers in front of Wallace, who read the headlines with satisfaction:

HUMANE PEST CONTROL TRIUMPHS AGAIN! RABBIT PROBLEM CONTAINED

"Another successful night, lad!" Wallace said contentedly. "How are the 'inmates'? Must be getting a bit full down there." His tummy growled hungrily. "Speaking of which, now for a great, big plate of . . ."

He looked down at the breakfast Gromit

had prepared for him. "Vegetables! Still got me on that diet, eh, Gromit? Ah, there's a good dog!" But vegetables were not what Wallace called a hearty breakfast. He was going to have to do something a little sneaky to get Gromit out of the way so he could fix himself a proper breakfast. "How's that prize marrow of yours coming on?" he asked Gromit.

As anticipated, Gromit trundled out to his greenhouse to measure his marrow. He had been tending it for months, with high hopes that, this year, he just might win the Giant Vegetable Competition.

Once Gromit was well out of sight, Wallace tipped the plate of vegetables down the rabbit-feeding chute before heading over to the bookshelves. He pressed a book entitled *Fromage to Eternity* and the whole bookshelf slid away to reveal a secret compartment full of cheese. Now *that's* what Wallace called the perfect breakfast!

He did so love cheese. He reached in excitedly but . . . SNAP!

"Aaaaaargh!" shouted Wallace.

Gromit heard the cry, but slowly finished what he was doing before going back to the dining room. He carefully removed the mousetrap from Wallace's red and swollen fingers.

"Oooh! Caught 'red-handed,' eh, lad!" Wallace laughed, but Gromit was not amused. "I'm sorry, Gromit. I'm just crackers about cheese!"

Gromit was clearly disappointed that his master couldn't keep his passion under control.

Wallace had an idea. "Look, if I must change me ways, at least let me do it my way—with technology," he said, pressing a pepper pot into the table to reveal a screen where his place mat had been. "It's time we tried my latest invention . . ."

A strange-looking helmet dropped down

from the ceiling. "The Mind-Manipulation-O-Matic!"

The machine clamped itself around Wallace's head and Gromit began to look worried.

"I haven't tested it yet, but it should be perfectly safe. Just a bit of harmless brain alteration." Wallace's hand reached out to the ON switch, but before he could press it the phone rang.

Gromit breathed a sigh of relief.

"Anti-pesto? . . . Ah, yes! Lady Tottington here, of Tottington Hall . . ." said the voice on the phone. "I have the most terrible rabbit problem. The competition is only days away. You simply have to do something!"

"Certainly, Ma'am!" Wallace said eagerly. "Just stay right where you are, your ladyship, and we'll be with you in an . . . *aaaaaargh*!"

Wallace had pressed the retract button for the helmet and it yanked him crashing up to the ceiling.

"An *aaar*!" Lady Tottington's posh voice resounded. "I can't wait an *aaar*. I have a major infestation!"

The doorbell rang at Tottington Hall. Relieved, Lady Tottington rushed to answer it. Her rabbit problem was a big worry.

But it wasn't Anti-pesto.

"What-ho!" said a rather pompous-looking gentleman standing at the door. He had a bunch of flowers in his hand and a brutish-looking hound by his side.

"Victor! How . . . lovely—and unexpected!" said Lady Tottington, rather taken aback.

"Heard you had a spot of rabbit bother and toodled straight on over to sort the little blighters out!" he snorted.

"Gosh—that's awfully sweet of you—but you really needn't—" Lady Tottington began.

"Don't want pests spoiling our beautiful manor house, do we?" said Victor, looking longingly at her impressive house.

"*Our* manor house? No one's mentioned marriage, Victor," she said quickly.

"All in good time, my dear. Vermin first, though." And he strode off with his dog, Philip, who had a large hunting rifle in his mouth.

"Victor!" Lady Tottington shouted after him. "We can deal with this . . . humanely!"

As Lady Tottington chased after Victor, the Anti-pesto van was approaching the house. Wallace marveled at its grandeur. It was about the size of ten ordinary houses—and heaven knows how long it would have taken to clean all those windows! This was going up in the world, all right.

The van skidded to a halt on the gravel and the dynamic duo leaped out. Using their bunny-catching grab, they immediately nabbed the pesky rabbit hopping around on Lady Tottington's lawn. Wallace stood up, looking very pleased with himself.

Anti-pesto had saved the day again. But his expression soon changed when he saw that the job was far from over—there were rabbits *everywhere*.

"You know what this means, don't you, lad?" he said to Gromit, who nodded his head and pressed a large red button on the dashboard of the van. Suddenly, feet shot out of the van and the sides dropped down to reveal a large glass machine inside—the Bun-Vac 6000.

On the other side of the house, Lady Tottington rushed up to Victor. "Haven't we agreed—no more thoughtless killing?"

Victor was aiming his rifle at a little bunny. He stopped.

"Quite right—so I've thought this one through very carefully!" he said, taking aim again.

"Victor, no!" But it was too late. Victor had fired his rifle.

At that precise moment, the rabbit in his gunsight was suddenly sucked into a nearby burrow and Victor's shot hit the ground where it had stood.

"What the . . . ?" exclaimed Victor, completely dumbfounded.

The rabbit was just as confused as Victor. Having been happily chomping grass just a few seconds ago, it was sucked into a rabbit hole and was now hurtling through a warren of tunnels with its eyes shut tight. Suddenly, the rabbit popped up into the glass storage tank of Anti-pesto's Bun-Vac 6000 and found itself floating in zero gravity. It was joined by countless other rabbits. Outside a face was staring in at them. "This'll impress her ladyship!" said Wallace proudly.

"I don't understand," cried Victor, staring down the rabbit hole. "Should have been a bullseye."

"Oh, Victor," sighed Lady Tottington. "I felt we'd made a real breakthrough with this hunting obsession. I really thought you'd changed."

He turned toward her. "I'm sorry, Companula, I am what I am." He knelt down and put his hand on his heart. "What you see is what you get!"

But, at that moment, Companula Tottington saw a little more of Victor than she'd ever seen before. The toupee that covered his bald spot was sucked clean from his head, and disappeared down the same rabbit hole as the rabbit. Acutely embarrassed, Victor leaped toward the hole and reached inside to retrieve the little wig, only to be sucked in himself.

A few seconds later, Victor's toupee was floating around the Bun-Vac chamber and the Bun-Vac 6000 began to strain.

"Sounds like a really big brute, this one," said Wallace. "Give it some more welly."

Gromit increased the machine's suck power.

At the other end of the tunnel, Victor disappeared into the hole and was sucked under the lawn. His dog, Philip, and Lady Tottington followed his trail above ground.

"Aah—Anti-pesto!" Lady Tottington cried as she approached the van. Wallace took one look at her and swooned. She was beautiful. He couldn't believe it when she spread out her arms toward him. What was he supposed to do? He awkwardly stretched his arms out too, puckered up his lips for a kiss and waited for her embrace, but she rushed straight past him.

"My darlings! You're safe!" she said to the rabbits in the Bun-Vac.

Gromit looked over at a very embarrassed Wallace.

"What a fabulous job you've done. And not a single one harmed," Lady Tottington cried gratefully. "Is this all of them?"

"Just one left, Lady Tottington! Hoist her up, Gromit."

Gromit pulled a lever that lifted the nozzle of the Bun-Vac out of the ground, only to find Victor stuck to the end of it. Gromit turned the machine off, and Victor landed in a dirty heap next to Lady Tottington.

"Victor!" she said excitedly. "The ingenious Anti-pesto has completely dealt with my rabbit problem. Isn't it marvelous?"

"Marvelous?" he bellowed. "This confounded contraption virtually suffocated me! And the job's only half done. How do you intend to finish these vermin off?"

"Victor! They're humane," she explained. "Anti-pesto is a pest savior, not murderer."

"Humane? Then perhaps they would be humane enough to give me back my dignity!"

Wallace didn't immediately take the hint.

"I want . . ." Victor lowered his voice and whispered to Wallace, ". . . toupee, please!"

"Oh, grand!" said Wallace, thinking he

wanted *to pay*. "We take checks or cash."

"Toupee, you idiot," Victor screeched. "My hair is in your machine."

Wallace was about to explain to him the difference between rabbits and hares, when Victor rudely pushed him aside and plunged his hand into the tank to retrieve his wig. He put it on his head and stormed off. The others watched him go.

Lady Tottington stifled a laugh when she saw that, instead of his wig, Victor had actually pulled a little black bunny from the Bun-Vac. It was sitting on his bald spot— waving good-bye.

A short time later, Wallace and Gromit were ready to leave Tottington Hall.

"Thank you for ridding me of a real problem, Wallace. Anti-pesto is a very smart outfit . . . I always did like a man in uniform," said Lady Tottington.

Wallace positively glowed with pride.

"What exactly will you do with all these rabbits?" inquired Lady Tottington.

"Oh." Wallace shot a look at Gromit. "Trade secret," he laughed nervously.

"I'd be happy to let them roam free, but they do so love their veggies! It's in their little bunny natures, and you can't change that, can you?" she laughed.

"No . . ." Wallace laughed along with her, but suddenly an idea was coming to him. He turned slowly to Gromit and said mysteriously, "Or can you?"

Chapter Three

In Wallace and Gromit's cellar, there were cages upon cages of rabbits. One of the rabbits was wearing Victor's toupee.

"We have to face up to it, lad, there are just too many rabbits," Wallace said later that night as they checked on the bunnies. "We can't keep 'em and we can't kill 'em. But what if we *could* alter their nature?"

He walked over to Gromit, who was sitting next to the Bun-Vac.

Then Wallace made a dramatic announcement. "Well, we *can*!" Pulling a chain, he released the cellar door so moonlight streamed in. "Simply by connecting the Bun-Vac to the Mind-Manipulation-O-Matic! Presto! Rabbit rehabilitation." It had occurred to Wallace that if he could alter the rabbits' brains to reject vegetables, the town's vegetables would be safe . . . forever! Gromit looked doubtful.

The Mind-O-Matic was connected to the Bun-Vac 6000 and everything was set to go. Wallace sat down and lowered the helmet on to his head. He pulled a lever and two lunar panels unfurled on the helmet, concentrating the lunar power into the helmet.

Wallace pressed a button and the helmet lit up and whirred to life.

Wallace began to emit his brain waves. "Veggies: bad. Veggies: bad . . ." he repeated. "Say no to carrots, cabbage, and cauliflower."

As instructed, Gromit reluctantly pressed the Bun-Vac lever to SUCK. The rabbits began to float around in the chamber. Wallace's brainwaves were being sucked from the

Mind-O-Matic helmet, up the attachment tube and down into the Bun-Vac.

"It's working, Gromit! Their tiny bunny brains are being saturated by my anti-veggie brainwaves. Another thirty minutes' brain-washing and we can move on to the conditioning."

Wallace relaxed and sat back in his chair. He picked up his newspaper and put up his feet—accidentally kicking the Bun-Vac switch to BLOW! Suddenly, all the rabbits in the Bun-Vac machine were blown up to the attachment tube, blocking the nozzle. One little rabbit got squeezed into the tube and was blown along toward the Mind-O-Matic helmet. Wallace panicked. Suddenly his brain waves were being mixed with the rabbit's.

"Groooomit! Quick! Switch it off," he yelled. But it seemed it might already be too late for Wallace, who was twitching and hopping round the cellar in great distress. Gromit grabbed a nearby wrench and

24

smashed the helmet to pieces.

Wallace sat up. He painfully extracted the petrified rabbit from his swollen head.

"Oooh, thanks, lad," he said, panting and exhausted. "Quick, give us a carrot!"

Not knowing what to make of this request, Gromit cautiously handed Wallace a carrot and was very relieved when Wallace immediately offered the carrot to the bunny. Disgusted, the bunny pushed it away.

"Ha! It worked, Gromit!" Wallace said delightedly. "A reformed rabbit! We'll call him Hutch, shall we?" He put Hutch into an empty cage. "He can soon be reintroduced back into the community."

Rubbing his head, Wallace walked off shakily, muttering about working on the rest of the rabbits tomorrow.

Gromit peered in at Hutch. He noticed Hutch twitch very strangely.

Later, Wallace finished adding Lady

Tottington's portrait to those of their most valued clients. Lady Tottington's Anti-pesto alarm was fitted and ready for action.

In his greenhouse, Gromit was tucking up his prize marrow in its electric blanket. All around the town, people were settling their vegetables down for the night and arming their Anti-pesto alarms.

A secure calm settled over the whole neighborhood, except in Wallace and Gromit's cellar. The rabbits all huddled together in the far corners of their cages, fearfully watching Hutch's hutch. It was shaking violently. Something peculiar was happening inside.

Across town, the vicar finished his prayer for the protection and nourishment of his beloved vegetables. He locked up his greenhouse for the night, picked up a basket of carrots, and carried them into the church. As he placed them on the harvest table with all the other delicious offerings from his congregation, he failed to notice that he'd been followed. Behind him, he heard heavy breathing in the darkness, then a long, low BURP!

"Mrs. Mulch?" he called. But there was no answer.

"Please—come forward. There's no need to be afraid," said the vicar calmly.

But the only response was a loud, salivating slurp from behind a pillar.

"You're hungry! Then, please—take what you like. It's for the needy, after all!"

But the vicar's calm benevolence turned to absolute horror as the "thing" rushed the table. He scrambled to find a crucifix with which to protect himself. All he managed to find were two cucumbers, which he crossed in front of him in desperation.

"MERCY!" he cried, but the cucumbers were the first things to be devoured. And that was just the start of the salivating beast's feeding frenzy. It ploughed through the harvest table full of vegetables in seconds and then smashed its way through a stained-glass window, heading toward the village gardens. No vegetable was safe from its furry clutches; no greenhouse or cold frame was secure against this . . . this . . . But what was it?

Chapter Four

The following morning, the town's gardeners were in an uproar. Everyone was gathered in the church and their angry shouts were directed at Wallace and Gromit, sitting red-faced in the middle of them all.

It had been a night like no other. The beast had rampaged through the town, ravaging innocent vegetables and leaving chaos and devastation in its wake.

The first Wallace and Gromit knew of this night of carnage was the following morning, when they found all the clients' portraits flashing. But why hadn't the Anti-pesto launch been activated? Gromit was the one who discovered the kettle—it had been mysteriously knocked from its ring on the stove, preventing its steam from turning the windmill on the Anti-pesto Wake-Up Device.

The newspaper headlines confirmed their fears. It was inconceivable but true. Anti-pesto had slept soundly through the worst night in West Wallaby's vegetable history.

"It's a disaster," someone in the crowd was shouting. "My garden's ruined."

"Where was Anti-pesto when we needed 'em?" questioned Mrs. Mulch.

"We pay good money for our crop protection!" trilled Miss Thripp.

"If you can't deliver the goods, maybe you should keep your traps shut!" said Mr. Crock, shoving a broken Anti-pesto trap into Wallace's lap. What could Wallace say or do?

PC Mackintosh tried to calm the growing tension. "That's enough! This flippin' vegetable competition causes nothing but trouble every year, what with jealous gardeners and the like . . ."

The crowd groaned. They had heard this before . . . until they were silenced by a chilling voice from the back of the hall.

"This was no *man*!" The voice was the vicar's. He moved up the aisle in his wheelchair, looking haunted and still feverish from his attack. "Does a man have teeth the size of axe blades?" he asked dramatically. "Or ears like terrible tombstones?"

He staggered to his feet and tottered slowly through the crowd, speaking like the tormented man he was.

"By tampering with nature, forcing vegetables to swell far beyond their natural size, we have brought a terrible judgement upon ourselves. And for our sins . . . a hideous creature has been sent to *punish* us all!"

The crowd gasped. PC Mackintosh shook his head, muttering. Even he felt chills running down his spine at the end of the vicar's sermon.

"Repent! Repent! Lest you too taste the wrath of . . . the WERE-RABBIT!"

Everyone turned to see what the vicar was pointing at—the frightening outline of a gigantic rabbit that had smashed through the church's stained-glass window.

Panic swept through the crowd. Wallace and Gromit could only gulp and exchange worried glances.

Someone asked the question on everyone's mind: "What's to become of the vegetable competition?"

Miss Thripp was desperate. "We live for that competition! It's all we have!" She looked imploringly at PC Mackintosh. "Who will save us?"

Suddenly, a gunshot rang out and everyone turned. There, with his smoking rifle in his hand, was Victor Quartermaine. His thug of a dog, Philip, was by his side. "A Were-rabbit? Come, come now," he scoffed. "I do believe the vicar's been at the communion wine again."

He reloaded his gun. "What we are dealing with here," he went on smugly, "is no supernatural rabbit! It's a big fellow perhaps, but flesh and blood. Easily dealt with by a hunter."

"Hasn't there been enough destruction?" a very posh voice rang out across the church. Lady Tottington was not going to let Victor kill anything, let alone a fluffy creature, however large. "I say we give Anti-pesto a second chance!" She gazed adoringly at Wallace, much to Victor's annoyance.

"How on earth would those tiny-minded buffoons ever catch such a big rabbit?" he scoffed.

Everyone looked at Wallace and he knew he had to come up with something good. Anti-pesto's reputation was at stake.

"Well . . ." he began, thinking very hard,

". . . with . . . a big trap!"

Gromit slapped his hand over his eyes. How could his master be so inadequate at a time like this?

"By Jove," said Mr. Crock, "he's got it!"

Then the whole church erupted in spontaneous applause. Once again, Victor had been upstaged, and he wasn't happy.

Later that evening, Wallace put his hasty but brilliant plan into action. The large trap he made was not a cage or a pit—but a huge and very lovely female rabbit, fixed to the top of the Anti-pesto van.

"Love, Gromit! That's the biggest trap of all, and that's what we'll use to catch this thing. How could any hot-blooded beast of a rabbit resist?"

Gromit was too busy to listen. While Wallace was driving, Gromit was in the back of the van, strings tied to his wrists and ankles, operating the rabbit on the roof like a puppeteer.

Wallace stuck his head out of the window to look at his giant creation. "Come on, Gromit," he yelled. "A bit more *alluring*."

Gromit did his best to do "alluring." He put his hand on his hips and wiggled—the female rabbit above him did the same. He pushed a pedal and the rabbit winked.

"That's more like it, lad," laughed Wallace, but he was paying more attention to what was above him than what was in front of him. They were heading toward a low bridge arch—far too low for the huge rabbit to fit through. She didn't stand a chance.

SMACK!

Unfortunately for Gromit, he was still attached by the strings. As the rabbit was torn from the van by the impact with the bridge, Gromit was violently yanked to the roof of the van, making an impression like a Jell-O mold.

Wallace slammed on his brakes as soon as he realized his clever plan was lying in a heap somewhere behind him. He got out of the van and went back through the arch to retrieve the lady rabbit. "Should fix back on quite easily . . ." he said as he disappeared from sight.

Gromit fell from the van's ceiling and watched Wallace go. He got in the front of the van and waited. The night felt strangely quiet and spooky. His unease grew as he realized he was sitting outside a greengrocer's shop, packed with tasty produce. He started to knit to calm his nerves, and turned up the radio. There was still no sign of Wallace.

Suddenly, the carrot sign that had been hanging outside the vegetable shop came crashing down on to the hood of the van—a giant-sized bite taken out of it. Something smashed the greengrocer's window and bounded off down the street, leaving a trail of half-eaten vegetables in its wake.

Gromit hooted the horn but, with no sign of Wallace, he started the van and gave chase. Although he could only see glimpses of giant furry paws and ears, Gromit pressed the giant lasso button on the van's dashboard. The lasso rope shot out of the front of the van and over the creature's neck. Gromit had caught it! But now the van was being dragged by the creature . . . over a hedge, into a park, and down a burrow!

Finding himself underground, Gromit's view was obscured by mud and vegetables being thrown at the van's windshield. All he could see was an enormous bunny tail and huge bunny feet. His windshield wipers were useless and the van was completely out of his control.

In her garden, Mrs. Girdling was locking her greenhouse. She turned to see a bulge underground, traveling at high speed toward her precious vegetables. She bellowed with rage, but there was no stopping the force of the underground menace. She frantically tried to protect whatever she could, but it burrowed directly under her greenhouse, and the whole thing, including Mrs. Girdling's vegetables, disappeared into the tunnel. It fell directly on to the Anti-pesto van, stopping it in its tracks and severing the lasso.

It was late the following morning before Gromit inched out of the rabbit tunnel. With a flick of the DE-MUD switch, the van shook itself clean. Gromit could now see that he was back home in his very own garden, but there was trouble here, too. The back door was smashed off its hinges and there were giant paw prints leading into the house.

Gromit followed the paw prints warily, but the first sound he heard was a very harrassed Wallace fielding complaints from clients on the telephone.

"Mrs. Girdling, now calm down. A tunnel,

you say? I'll look into it . . ."

He put the phone down and pulled the plug on all the alarms flashing around him.

"So where did you get to, lad?" he said to Gromit. "It's gone mad! I thought we were supposed to be a team?"

But Gromit's attention was still firmly fixed on the monster-sized paw prints leading to the wide-open cellar door.

Bravely, he descended the cellar stairs. Wallace followed, still moaning. "How is this sort of behavior going to get us any closer to finding a rabbit monster . . .?" He stopped when he saw the smashed-up cage, with Hutch squatting awkwardly inside.

They looked at each other with growing realization. Wallace looked over to the broken Mind-O-Matic machine.

"Hutch! Hutch is the beast! The lunar panels . . . They must have overstimulated Hutch's primitive bunny nature—and now when the moon appears, he undergoes a hideous transformation . . ." It was a chilling discovery. "Oh, this is absolutely . . . FANTASTIC!"

What? Gromit looked confused.

"Don't you see, lad! Okay, so we've created a veggie-ravaging rabbit monster—but we've also captured it!" And with that, he hurried off to break the good news to Lady Tottington.

Gromit hastily made a special, reinforced cage for Hutch. Lastly, he locked the cellar door and put a plank across it so there was no way that Hutch could escape. With his work done, Gromit relaxed . . . only to notice that the muddy paw prints that had led him into the house continued *past* the cellar door. Gromit followed them up the stairs. They gradually turned from rabbit-shaped paw prints to man-shaped footprints—and they led into *Wallace's* bedroom. With only a moment's hesitation, Gromit opened the bed-room door. The sight that greeted him was horrific—Wallace's bed was littered with half-devoured vegetables and oversized rabbit droppings. Immediately, Gromit knew what he was dealing with. He had to find Wallace . . . and fast!

Chapter Five

It was Lady Tottington herself who answered the door.

"It's the beast, your ladyship. I bring great news!" Wallace told her.

"Gosh, how exciting. Do come in!"

Wallace stomped his foot like a rabbit and bounded into the house. Over tea, Wallace told Lady Tottington all about Hutch, now securely caged in his basement.

"Simply spiffing!" Lady Tottington was truly delighted. "With the beast in captivity, the competition can go ahead. You've saved the day, Mr. Wallace." She stood up. "Please help yourself," she said, gesturing to a plate of cookies. As she turned away, Wallace helped himself to a tasty-looking flower in a vase, ignoring the cookies altogether. "Tell me," Lady Tottington smiled at him, "are you a vegetable lover yourself?"

"They're growing on me," Wallace answered truthfully.

"Then come with me." She led Wallace to a small elevator. "Hop in!" she said. Wallace hopped.

Gromit raced to Tottington Hall in the van. He watched as Wallace and Lady Tottington disappeared into the elevator up to a large rooftop conservatory that crowned the stately home.

"Welcome to my secret garden," Lady Tottington announced.

Wallace was mesmerized—he was

surrounded by a feast of plump vegetables.

"It's a veritable vegetable paradise!" Wallace exclaimed.

Lady Tottington was delighted that she had found someone who truly appreciated her passion. She was feeling a warmth between them and she moved closer to Wallace. Neither of them noticed Gromit's face suddenly appearing at the window.

Gromit saw how potentially dangerous this situation was—if he was right and Wallace was the Were-rabbit, he knew there could be carnage. Lady Tottington's sumptuous vegetables were in danger. And the day was drawing to an end. When the moon rose, Wallace would soon turn into the beast. Gromit had to do something.

Just as Lady Tottington was tempting Wallace beyond rabbit resistance by thrusting the largest, most delicious-looking carrot under his nose, Gromit had an idea. The sprinkler system was his only hope: He

Victor thinks the only way to get rid of the ravenous rabbit is to shoot it.

Wallace and Gromit think they've found the culprit.

The Mind-Manipulation-O-Matic has gone
horribly wrong.

Gromit helps the Were-rabbit escape.

Victor can't believe his eyes.

There is chaos at the Giant Vegetable Competition!

The Were-rabbit grabs Lady Tottington!

Who or what will save the day?

launched an asparagus spear and activated the sprinkler system lever . . .

Wallace was dripping wet and VERY cross.

"I don't know what that was about, Gromit, but it certainly wasn't funny OR clever! Ruined a perfectly good tank top, to say nothing of a relationship with an important client." His grumbling didn't stop, even when they came to a surprising diversion in the road as they drove home. The sun was setting and Gromit stepped on the gas, driving faster and deeper into the woods.

Suddenly, Gromit had to slam on the brakes. A tree trunk was blocking the road. Gromit saw that it had been deliberately felled.

"This is all I need . . ." Wallace grumbled as he got out, then tried to move the heavy tree.

Out of the corner of his eye, Gromit saw

a glint of metal just before an axe flew past Wallace's head and embedded itself in the tree. Out of the shadows stepped Victor and Philip.

"I know your little secret, Pesto," Victor sneered. He had been to Tottington Hall and watched as Lady Tottington invited Wallace up to her rooftop greenhouse. "You think you can pilfer my filly, don't you?"

Wallace was puzzled.

"Think you can con an innocent woman out of her fortune? Well, I GOT THERE FIRST! I've spent a long time reeling in that fluffy-headed bunny lover and I'm not about to let some pitiful little peasant poach her from me."

"Righto," said Wallace, trying to escape. "I'll be off, then." But his suspenders were pinned to the tree by the axe.

Victor rolled up his sleeves. "You're not going anywhere—not until I've taught you a lesson."

Gromit tried to get out of the van to help, but Philip was holding the door shut, shaking his head at him. Gromit soon changed his mind about wanting to help. Wallace was trembling and shaking all over—but it wasn't from fear. The moon had come out and the lunar rays were triggering off the transformation. Gromit hastily locked the van's doors. He knew what was about to happen.

As Victor threw his first punch, his fist was stopped in mid-flight by a giant hairy paw. The next moment, he was hurtling through the air and landed hard on the van's hood. Philip desperately tried to get into the van, but this time it was Gromit who shook his head at Philip.

All they could do was watch in horror as Wallace's teeth became the size of axe blades and furry ears grew out of his head. The beast was once again at large!

Tossing the tree trunk out of the way, the

beast let out an almighty howl, echoed by a tribe of little rabbits in the woods around. Then it bounded off at a breakneck hop. Cowering under the van, Victor and Philip stared after the beast, frozen in shock and disbelief.

Gromit pulled himself together and fired up the van—he needed to find his master. But he didn't have a clue what he was going to do when he'd found him!

A fearsome storm had descended over West Wallaby. Lightning flashes lit up the night sky and thunderclaps rattled every window. It was not a night to be out, but someone was hammering on the vicarage door. The vicar hurried to answer it and there stood Victor. "I want to talk to you. About the beast," he explained.

The vicar, still a little twitchy after his experience in the church, showed Victor into his study. "Everything you need to know is in here," he said, placing a dusty old book in front of Victor. It was a book of monsters. Inside, they were all there—the Loch Ness Monster, Big Foot, and the notorious Were-cow. Finally, they came to THE WERE-RABBIT, with a picture of what Wallace had now become.

"So, you were right!" exclaimed Victor. "Tell me, how do I kill him? . . . I mean *it*."

"To kill such a creature would require nerves of steel and—" he hesitated as the storm raged—"a bullet of pure gold!"

"Gold?" Victor questioned. But the vicar was already opening a dark cupboard to show Victor his arsenal of monster-defeating weapons. There were wooden stakes, crosses, garlic and . . . three golden bullets.

"Twenty-four karat!" the vicar cackled.

"Oh, get out of my way, you silly old fool." Shoving the vicar aside, Victor grabbed the bullets.

The vicar had seen a frightening look in

Victor's eyes. "Beware the beast within!" he called after him.

Victor responded with an evil chuckle. "Oh, no, this particular beast is *without*—without a chance that is."

Chapter Six

"BEAST STRIKES AGAIN!" blared the headlines in the morning paper. Gromit read them with anguish, then pulled the Get-U-Up lever to get Wallace out of bed. The trapdoor opened and out dropped a stream of half-eaten vegetables, followed by a relatively normal-looking Wallace. Except that he still had two huge, floppy, furry ears!

"This vegetable diet's doing the trick, eh, lad?" Wallace said, patting his new slimline tummy. It was the first time he had slid through the Get-U-Up trapdoor without the help of a mallet. He picked up his carrot breakfast. "So, how's our rabbit monster? Hope you're keeping an eye on him!"

Gromit could do nothing but stare. BOTH eyes were firmly fixed on Wallace.

"What's up, dog? You look as if you've seen a ghost." At this, Gromit picked up a mirror and held it up to Wallace's face—and his ears, which straightened in shock.

"Well, fancy that! Rabbit ears. That is a bit odd," said Wallace, not quite grasping the situation.

Gromit pointed to the newspaper photo of the beast.

"What? No. You think I'm the . . . What, because of these?" he laughed, pointing to his new ears. "Oh, no. This is just a . . ." he was beginning to struggle . . . "a reaction to that vegetable diet. It's the 'toxins' coming out!" He patted Gromit on the head patronizingly. "Silly old pooch! Next you'll be saying Hutch is turning into me. Ha!"

Gromit hadn't thought of that, but what a

52

scary idea! He went down to the cellar and carefully lowered the door to Hutch's cage. Wallace was behind him, looking on anxiously.

"What are you doing, lad?" he said. "Have you gone completely mad?" But Gromit just held out a wedge of Wallace's favorite food in his hand.

From the depths of the cage came a high-pitched Wallacelike cry. "Cheeeeeeeese!" And out of the cage stepped Hutch, in slippers, a tank top, and looking extremely Wallacelike.

"That's just grand!" Hutch said, and wolfed down the cheese.

Wallace couldn't escape the grim truth any longer. Hutch *was* turning into him, and he must be turning into . . . well, the rabbit beast! Wallace was HORRIFIED!

Oblivious to the turmoil across town, Lady Tottington was gaily preparing for the competition. "Come along, we've got a show to get ready!" she announced to the workmen erecting the bunting and the bouncy castle.

She lovingly dusted the coveted Golden Carrot Award to be presented to the grower of the most magnificent vegetable. "It's going to be such a jolly competition," she warbled.

"How can it be," asked Mrs. Mulch, "when the beast is still out there?"

"Mrs. Mulch!" said Lady Tottington, rather taken aback. "Mr. Wallace told me—"

"A pack of lies!" interrupted Mr. Windfall. "Look at my brassicas," he said, "ravaged in the night!"

"It's not safe to bring our veggies here. The show's off!" announced Mr. Caliche.

Lady Tottington couldn't believe her eyes or her ears. She had trusted Wallace completely. She thought they had an understanding. And now, for the first time in five hundred years, the Giant Vegetable

Competition was in jeopardy. Was there no one who could save it?

Suddenly, several shots rang out, knocking down the bunnies in the shooting gallery. It was Victor, and his gun.

"Heard you had a spot of rabbit bother . . ."

Lady Tottington found herself wrestling with her conscience. Should she put family tradition before animal protection and let Victor shoot the beast? It was a dilemma she could hardly bear.

Later that day, Wallace was down in the cellar, feverishly trying to reassemble the Mind-O-Matic machine. Dusk was approaching.

"Shouldn't take long . . . Just mend the Mind-O-Matic, reverse the process, and I'll be a happy bunny. I mean . . . not a bunny at all!" Then his altered mind started to play tricks on him. As he picked up a discombobulator (a part of the machine), it seemed to turn into a delicious carrot—he just *had* to have a nibble.

"Oh, it's hopeless!" he said despairingly, throwing the part down in disgust at himself. "Me mind's just a rabbitty mush. I'll never fix the flippin' thing," Wallace wailed. "I don't want to be a rabbit, Gromit. I'll have to go underground . . . No! That's the worst thing I can do!" He burst into tears.

Suddenly, the doorbell rang. Wallace's ears pricked up.

"I can't answer the door," he said in a panic. But Hutch had no such problem. He was off up the stairs, looking and behaving every bit like Wallace.

Wallace bounded after him, with Gromit following closely behind.

"Ho, ho, no more lodgers, eh, lad!" called out Hutch as he went to open the door. There stood Lady Tottington.

Gromit grabbed Hutch and pulled him back inside. Wallace, with a winter hat on his head to conceal his rabbit ears, took Hutch's place at the door.

"Wallace?" said a very confused Lady Tottington. "I'm afraid I have some rather bad news. The thing is . . . you've rather let me down. It's quite obvious you have absolutely no idea where this poor creature is."

Wallace and Gromit both knew otherwise but they couldn't say anything. "I'm afraid you've given me no option . . ." She was getting tearful. "I've agreed to let Victor shoot the poor thing."

"Shoot it?" said Wallace slowly.

"Yes. It wasn't an easy choice, but the vegetable competition has to come first. Besides, Victor's promised me it won't suffer."

Wallace wasn't really listening. He could feel his hat lifting off his head. He hastily pulled it down and realized that the moon was rising. He fastened the hat under his chin, only to discover his hand was growing fur. His feet were soon to follow.

"I cannot deny it was a difficult decision," Lady Tottington went on, fortunately unable to look Wallace in the eye. "I've recently developed . . . *feelings* for you."

Even though Lady Tottington was pouring her heart out—and to a normal Wallace this would have filled him with pure joy—he just couldn't concentrate. He now had four furry paws and was struggling to keep his face under control.

"Feelings?" he said. "Oh well, never mind, eh. Ta-ta, then."

He tried to shut the door but Lady Tottington was not ready to walk away from him just yet.

"Wallace, I haven't finished yet. There's so much more that needs to be said . . ." She felt helpless. She was so convinced the feelings she felt were mutual. She'd seen it in his eyes.

"It's not very convenient at the moment. Thanks for coming, bye!" Wallace said hurriedly, slamming the door in her face.

Lady Tottington stood dejected on the other side of the door, her bottom lip trembling. She slowly walked away, turning one last time, unable to comprehend what had just happened. And there was Wallace at the window, pulling stupid faces as he transformed. Insulted and upset, she set off down the street, sobbing her heart out.

From the shadows, Victor watched her go. "That's right, my lovely. You can say good-bye to your fluffy lover boy!" He loaded his rifle with one of the golden bullets from his gun belt and strode toward Wallace's house.

Inside, Wallace was beside himself. "You've got to help me, Gromit . . ." he gasped, feeling his teeth growing, ". . . before it's too late." And with that his hat flew off, revealing his rabbit ears, and his nose instantly changed into a rabbit's nose.

Through the glass in the door, Gromit saw

Victor outside. He grabbed Wallace, in mid-transformation, and dragged him toward the garden. He was almost out when the final stage of the transformation happened—Wallace's huge rabbit bottom and tail wedged him in the door. Now fully transformed, all his rabbit instincts were in place and the need for carrots made him oblivious to impending danger. Wallace the Were-rabbit bounded back into the house to the carrot cupboard.

Munching away, his attention was suddenly distracted by the sound of a wolf whistle coming from the garden. Turning around he saw a very fine, very alluring lady rabbit standing at the back door. And she was just his size!

Gromit had been quick to act. He knew there was only one rabbit instinct stronger than carrot-hunger—love—and he'd remembered that the abandoned lady-rabbit decoy was still in the garden from their previous attempt at luring the beast. And this time it worked! The Were-rabbit was very interested and moved fast toward the bunny bait.

Inside the bunny suit, Gromit leaped into action. Seeing a hopping ball, he jumped on it and bounced into the next-door garden, just as Victor kicked down the front door, his rifle at the ready. The beast bounced enthusiastically after the lady bunny, so when Victor arrived in the back garden, he could only just see the shape of a giant rabbit hopping over the garden fences. Victor, with the instincts of a hunter, quickly raised his rifle and fired. CRACK! He smiled as he saw the shape of a big rabbit tumble down behind a fence.

The sound of the shot rang out across the town and all the way to Tottington Hall. The assembled crowd heard the resulting howl.

"'Tis done," said Mr. Growbag solemnly.

Lady Tottington burst into tears. She had

given Victor permission to commit this murder and she felt dreadful.

"My poor, sensitive child," sympathized the vicar. "Allow us all to share . . . in your moment of sorrow." He slowly turned toward the crowd, raised his watery eyes and with sheer glee shouted, "YES! On with the show!"

The crowd cheered and the fireworks exploded. The Great Vegetable Competition could go ahead without fear of the beast! Or so they thought.

Victor strode over to his "kill." His competitor for Lady Tottington's hand in marriage—and her riches—was dead, once and for all. He lifted up the giant rabbit's head . . . but it came away in his hand! He was left holding the head of a huge, handmade female rabbit!

Gromit peeked out from inside the rabbit's body.

"Why, you . . .!" Victor snarled. He lifted

his rifle again, but his precious golden bullets could not be wasted on a measly mutt. "Your loyalty is moving . . . unlike you!" He slammed Gromit into an Anti-pesto trap and locked it.

"Come along, Philip," Victor sneered. "Everyone's been looking forward to a good show. Let's see they get one!" Sniggering, they left Gromit and set off in the direction of their real prey. Victor knew where it was heading—to the tastiest vegetable feast in town, the Giant Vegetable Competition at Tottington Hall.

With an explosion of fireworks, the Annual Tottington Vegetable Fair had officially begun. The Bag-a-Bunny shooting gallery was proving hugely popular—the townsfolk all expressing their anger and frustration by blowing away every bunny target on the stand . . . *and* the fluffy-bunny prizes.

The vicar struggled through the crowd with

his prize eggplant and headed toward the competition table. PC Mackintosh was there, trying to maintain some kind of order among the worryingly competitive townsfolk.

"All right, all right, don't crowd the table!" he hollered through his megaphone. "If we must do this flippin' veggie show, let's do it in an orderly fashion. Lettuces give way to marrows. Carrots—wait your turn!" He stopped. "Hey, you! A tomato isn't actually a vegetable. It's a fruit. You're disqualified."

Sneaking behind all the tents was Victor, trying to keep out of sight and still hunting for the beast. The prize veggies were just the bait he needed to lure the beast into his rifle sights. All he had to do was wait for the fluffy fiend to show up. It was Mrs. Girdling who blew his cover.

"Hey, look, everyone—it's Victor!" she cried.

"Our hero!" everyone chorused.

Victor looked uncomfortable as he strode

out into the adoring crowd. "Yes, thank you. Very nice, yes." Only he—and the beast—knew he hadn't yet earned this adoration. Suddenly, his eyes settled on a vision of carrot loveliness. Lady Tottington, dressed for the occasion in a hat and dress of the brightest orange, looked almost edible!

"Victor, give it to me straight. Did it suffer?"

"Of course not, my dear!" he mumbled, hurrying away. "Not yet, anyway!" he said under his breath.

Victor needed PC Mackintosh to help him organize the crowd. He sidled up to him.

"Um, Constable . . ." he said discreetly, not wanting anyone else to hear, "I don't want to panic anyone, but the beast isn't actually dead yet . . ."

But PC Mackintosh wasn't the brightest policeman in the world and, alarmed, he repeated at loudspeaker volume, "THE BEAST ISN'T ACTUALLY DEAD YET?"

Victor tried to shush him, but it was no use. The crowd heard every chilling word, and the whole fair came to a grinding halt. There was a moment of total silence . . . then COMPLETE AND UTTER PANIC!

"To the competition stand. We must save our veggies!" called a voice.

"Doomed, doomed! Your vegetables are all doomed!" wailed the vicar.

At West Wallaby Street Gromit picked up an old trowel and tried to force the lock of the trap, but it was no use. Those traps did their job too well. It was inescapable.

"Good night, Gromit!" came a familiar voice, a faint call from the bedroom of Wallace and Gromit's house.

It was Hutch! And sounding more than ever like a miniaturized Wallace. Why hadn't Gromit thought of him before? There was hope. Gromit quickly formed a plan. Seeing an Anti-pesto Gnome Alarm near the cage, he threw the trowel handle at it.

For a second nothing happened and Gromit held his breath, then BEEP, BEEP, BEEP. The alarm was activated and all Gromit had to do was wait.

Sure enough, Hutch was sitting up in bed, about to treat himself to an enormous chunk of Wensleydale when the alarm flashed in the house. Suddenly, the bed tipped up and the Anti-pesto launch began. Hutch found himself hurtling down the launch chute. The system wasn't designed for such a small rabbit and so it was a rather ruffled and bizarrely dressed Hutch who finally fell into the Anti-pesto van, looking not-so-ready for action. He couldn't even see over the steering wheel, but he crunched the van into reverse gear and smashed through the rear wall of the garage and into the Anti-pesto cage, freeing Gromit.

"Job well done, lad," said Hutch, sticking his head out of the window.

But before they left, Gromit made a decision. With a heavy heart, he looked lovingly at his marrow nestling cozily in his greenhouse, and knew what he had to do.

Chapter Seven

At the Giant Vegetable Competition, there was a stampede to the competition stand. Victor slapped his head—he had to stop this mayhem. He fired a shot into the air. "Quiet. QUIET!" he shouted. The mob stopped in their tracks. "Yes, the beast is here somewhere, but listen carefully. I've only got two—" He rolled his eyes, remembering the shot he'd just fired. "I mean ONE golden bullet left, so let me handle this. Your prize vegetables are the perfect bait and will draw the creature like a magnet. I need each and every one of you to keep perfectly still.

Don't flinch. Don't even move a muscle . . ."

All eyes were on Victor. The tension was too much.

Suddenly, Mrs. Mulch broke cover and made a run for it.

"Mrs. Mulch! No!" cried Lady Tottington.

"It's not gettin' my baby," Mrs. Mulch shouted tearfully, frantically pushing her precious pumpkin away in its pram.

The crowd shouted in chorus, "Come back! Come back, Mrs. Mulch!"

Almost immediately, the ground started to shake. The beast was there, but *under* the ground.

"Right on cue," beamed Victor.

"Noooo!" shouted Mr. Mulch as he quickly realized that the trail of the underground beast was gaining on his wife. Meanwhile, Mrs. Mulch had changed her mind and turned round. Now she was speeding back toward the competition stand.

Everyone looked on in horror and all except

Mr. Mulch changed their tune and shouted, "Go away! Go away, Mrs. Mulch!" But the beast had overtaken her and was heading straight at the vegetable stand, hungry for its dinner.

"Shoot it! Shoot it, your lordship! Please!" cried a voice in the crowd.

Victor smiled evilly. "Come to Victor," he muttered under his breath. One bullet left; he had to make it count.

But when the mound drew closer there was a sudden flash of green as something swept into the path of the beast, making it suddenly veer off course.

"Curses!" spat Victor.

The crowd was frantic. People tried to grab Victor's gun, which went off, and the last golden bullet ricocheted harmlessly off the speeding Anti-pesto van.

It was Gromit who had come to the beast's rescue, astride his prize marrow like a rodeo rider, pulled along behind the

Anti-pesto van driven by Hutch. They had used the delicious-smelling vegetable to lure Wallace the Were-rabbit away from the competition stand just in time.

"That's champion!" Hutch called from the wheel of the van as they successfully enticed the beast farther away from the competition stand.

"Hooray for Anti-pesto!" called Lady Tottington.

"I need more gold bullets," cried Victor, frantically scanning around him. Then he caught sight of three things that would make the ultimate weapon—the Golden Carrot Award shining on its stand, a box of fireworks, and an old blunderbuss on an antiques stall. Pouring gunpowder from the fireworks into the blunderbuss, Victor grabbed the Golden Carrot.

"No, Victor! What are you doing?" squealed Lady Tottington.

"I need it, my sweet! Emergency!"

shouted Victor.

"But it's my Golden Carrot Award," wailed Lady Tottington, trying to wrestle it away from Victor's clutches. It was her pride and joy.

"The Golden Carrot belongs in the show," insisted Lady Tottington.

"No, the Golden Carrot belongs in the Were-rabbit!" yelled Victor. "Let go!"

"No, Victor. Stop it! Stop it!" Her sobs of distress resounded across the fairground and reached the ears of the Were-rabbit. It immediately stopped in its tracks and looked to where Victor was grappling with Lady Tottington. A Wallacelike look of rage came over the beast. It forgot about chasing after Gromit and the marrow, and made off toward the stand to help Lady Tottington.

The garden-supplies stall was suddenly mobbed as the crowd armed themselves with pitchforks, shovels, and rakes. Mrs. Mulch grabbed herself a hedge-trimmer. It was payback time!

Having taken his eyes off his prey for a second to load the Golden Carrot into the blunderbuss, Victor looked up to see the van veering out of control and finally crashing into the cheese tent. There was no sign of the beast.

There was a gentle tap on Victor's shoulder. He turned round slowly to see the beast towering over him. Furious at Victor's treatment of Lady Tottington, the Were-rabbit bopped him on the head, wrecked his wig, and threw him into a cotton-candy maker. Then it tenderly picked up Lady Tottington to carry her away to safety.

But the crowd was turning ugly, even uglier than it had been to begin with. The people had the Were-rabbit cornered in seconds. There was only one way it could escape—and that was up. Still clutching Lady Tottington, the Were-rabbit leaped up and scaled the wall of Tottington Hall.

"Help!" shrieked Lady Tottington.

"Somebody help me!"

In the cheese tent Gromit picked himself up from the pieces that remained of his precious marrow. But he had no time to be upset. He looked out of the tent door toward all the commotion. And there was Victor, his bald head shining, as he scrambled up a drainpipe in pursuit of the beast, still clutching the blunderbuss with its lethal bullet inside.

Gromit knew he must act. He set off for the Hall but his path was immediately blocked by Philip, growling menacingly. Over Philip's shoulder he could see the drainpipe give way under Victor's weight. He bellowed as the pipe swung down, dropping him head-first into the cotton-candy machine. It was just enough of a distraction for Gromit to give Philip the slip. But he knew Philip was a hunting dog and would soon be on his tail.

Up in the Hall's rooftop conservatory a

terrified Companula Tottington said, "Put me down, you . . . you . . . whatever you are."

The beast set Lady Tottington down gently.

"What are you staring at with those beastly eyes?" she cried, but her hysteria soon waned as she looked at the Were-rabbit's face more closely. It was looking sorrowful, almost apologetic. "What are you trying to tell me?" she asked softly.

The Were-rabbit gave her a little Wallace wave.

"Wallace?" she said, slowly realizing just who this was in front of her.

Dodging behind a tent, Gromit had spotted a sign: "Reach for the Skies . . ." It was a ride with battery-powered airplanes and it gave him an idea. He stuffed a whole stack of coins into one of the little planes and it powered off in pursuit of Victor. But before long, Philip was in another one of the planes, chasing Gromit hard toward the helter-skelter slide! Now Gromit could see that the ride's full title was "Reach for the Skies . . . the Ultimate Dogfight."

In the conservatory Lady Tottington stroked the big furry beast. "Oh, Wallace! Whatever have you done to yourself?" The tenderness had crept back into her voice. "Well, don't worry. I'll protect you. You can stay here at Tottington Hall; there's plenty of room in the east wing."

At that moment, the lift to the conservatory pinged. "Get your hairy mitts off my future wife, you big brute!" It was Victor, his wig replaced by a swirl of pink cotton candy and the blunderbuss pointing directly at Wallace.

"No, Victor, you mustn't shoot. It's—"

"An extremely dangerous animal, my love! Now stand aside," commanded Victor. "You commissioned me to rid you of Pesto and that's just what I intend to do."

"Pesto? You mean . . ." gasped Lady

Tottington, realization dawning.

"Er . . . Pest! I meant 'pest'," mumbled Victor.

"Victor, you knew it was Wallace all along!" Suddenly, she could see through all that fake charm and exaggerated affection.

"All right, so what if it is that blithering idiot—no one will ever believe you. And a hunter always gets his prey!" Victor raised the blunderbuss.

And outside, as Gromit drove the little plane faster and faster up the helter-skelter slide, he could see the silhouette of Victor raising his gun—he must hurry.

But Companula Tottington was no pushover. "To think I might have married you. *You're* the only monster around here!" she shrilled. Grabbing some pansy spray, she squirted it into Victor's eyes. "Run, rabbit. Run!" she cried to the Wallace-beast as Victor blubbed like a toddler.

The beast crashed out through the glass

and made off over the roof.

Philip was right behind Gromit as they reached the top of the helter-skelter slide and both planes were launched into the air. They soared high above the heads of the crowd before landing safely on a wide ledge on the side of Tottington Hall. The ensuing battle became a real and very vicious dogfight.

In the conservatory, Victor was furious. He picked up a two-pronged pitchfork and launched it at Lady Tottington, pinning her hair to the wall.

"I rather like your hair pinned back," said Victor with a smirk. Then he turned to see the beast disappearing over the rooftops. He leaped after it, his hunter's instincts at full pitch. "You can hop but you can't hide, Pesto!"

But now Gromit had Victor in his sights. He drove his little plane directly at Victor from behind. Just as he was about to buffet the pink-headed toff from the rooftops, Philip caught up and rammed Gromit's plane. Gromit veered wildly off course and just missed Victor, who staggered right into the path of Philip's plane. It butted him right in the behind, sending him somersaulting through the air. Victor was lucky enough to be hooked by his belt on the arrow of a weather vane.

With increasing speed, Philip chased Gromit's plane along the length of the ledge, getting closer and closer, until he managed to ram Gromit again. Gromit put on a spurt and led the chase up to a higher ledge.

Victor had wriggled himself free from the weather vane and now he was really mad. He could see the beast scrabbling around at the edge of the roof . . . there was nowhere for it to go.

Now Philip had caught up with Gromit again, his propeller chewing into the back of Gromit's plane. Gromit rounded a corner at high speed and looked back. Philip was no longer behind him. Suddenly, Philip appeared *in front* of Gromit and headed straight for him! A horrible collision was inevitable but Gromit held his nerve. At the last second it was Philip's plane that swerved off course to avoid the crash, and went spiralling down toward the ground. One down; now for the real villain.

Gromit looked up to see Victor approaching the beast. He was very close now. Gromit steered his plane toward Victor. But as he closed in, Gromit suddenly realized he wasn't alone in his little plane! From nowhere, Philip had popped up and he grabbed Gromit from behind. They started to fight and Philip wrenched an axe from a coat of arms. Just when it looked like the end for Gromit, he found the lever in the plane for the bomb doors and yanked it. The doors opened and Philip fell through, plummeting down on to the bouncy castle, which crumpled and hissed as Philip's teeth punctured it.

Still flying high, Gromit could see the terrified Were-rabbit cornered against a turret. There was no escape, and Victor was closing in on him. Victor had all the time in the world to aim his shot, and there was no way he was going to miss.

"Now to finish the job!" he said. "Eat carrot, bunny boy!"

As Victor fired the Golden Carrot from the blunderbuss, Gromit grabbed hold of a TV antenna and swung the plane round. It was a moment of precise timing. The plane took the full force of the golden bullet, right in its side. Wallace was saved! There were cheers from a little crowd of bunnies who had watched the whole thing from the edge of the fair.

Victor was furious and immediately flew into a toddler tantrum. "Oh, potty poohs!" he yelled and stamped his feet with frustration.

Gromit couldn't hold on to the TV antenna any longer. He let go and his plane fell from the sky. The Wallace within the Were-rabbit saw what was happening and heroically dived out to grab hold of Gromit. They plunged from the roof together, falling down through the night and ripping right through the roof of the cheese tent, flattening the cheese stalls.

High on the roof, Victor changed his tune. "Hah! No one beats Victor Quartermaine!" he bellowed.

"Is that so?" said a voice behind him. It was Lady Tottington. She whacked him as hard on the head as she could with her prize Golden Carrot. "Oh, by the way . . ." she said, ". . . the marriage is off!" Victor teetered and fell, also landing in the cheese tent.

Gromit was the first to come around. He could hear the mob outside the tent. "The beast is in there! Let's get him."

"Stand aside!" bellowed Mrs. Mulch with

her hedge-cutter. "I'm going in!"

With Wallace still unconscious under the cheese stall, Gromit had to do something, and fast! He quickly zipped a dazed and groggy Victor into the lady-rabbit suit and kicked him out of the tent. Victor was the perfect Were-rabbit decoy. Mrs. Mulch stopped in her tracks. Towering above her was the hugest rabbit she'd ever seen. Philip, trained to hunt and not ask too many questions, sank his teeth into his master's giant furry bottom.

"Aaaaaargh!" Victor shrieked.

"It's the beast! See how it rages, hear how he roars! After it!" yelled the crowd. And everyone chased Victor in his bunny suit right out of the fair and into the woods. Lady Tottington rushed to the cheese tent and watched the crowd disappear into the distance.

"Let's see how he likes being hunted," she said, looking very satisfied. She turned back to see a distraught Gromit keeping vigil over his master, who had not moved since the fall. Little rabbit faces peered in under the tent flaps, shedding little rabbit tears.

"Oh, Gromit. Only a miracle could save him now," Lady Tottington said, wiping her eye. Gromit's eyes filled with tears and he put his head on his master's furry body. He loved Wallace, bunny ears or no bunny ears. A dog without his master was like the night without day, a bird without a song, Wallace without cheese . . .

Of course! Cheese. It was the thing that always woke Wallace from a deep sleep. Hutch had been sneakily filling a plate with the most stinky cheese he could find, ready for a huge cheese feast. Gromit grabbed his plate and wafted it under Wallace's nose. The movement was barely noticeable at first, but Wallace's nose was definitely twitching. He was alive! And he was becoming human again!

"Hmm. Cheese! Where am I?" Realizing he wasn't in cheese heaven, Wallace slowly took everything in. "Gromit! Well done, old pal. You clever pooch. You did it!"

Wallace got up and danced around, giving Gromit a massive excitable hug.

"Wallace! You're all . . . oooh!" Lady Tottington raised her eyebrows and blushed.

Wallace looked down, and hastily covered his modesty.

Lady Tottington tittered mischievously and then she picked up the battered Golden Carrot and presented it to Gromit, saying, "I think you deserve this, Gromit. For a very brave and splendid marrow."

Gromit was very happy and Wallace beamed. "Every dog has his day, eh, lad?"

"And thank you, Wallace," said Lady Tottington, smiling. "You saved me from a terrible marriage." She gave a little sigh. "Still, it is going to be rather lonely at Tottington Hall now—unless . . ." She shuffled her feet and looked rather embarrassed. "Wallace, I have a little proposal . . ."

Chapter Eight

The sun shone brightly on Tottington Hall as Wallace and Lady Tottington appeared at the front door of the magnificent hall.

"Oh, Wallace! I'm so thrilled you agreed to this!" said Lady Tottington.

"My pleasure," replied Wallace. "Shall we get on with it, then?"

With a nod, Lady Tottington reached up and pulled on a long cord. A curtain slowly opened to reveal a shiny brass plaque. The wording on the sign said:

TOTTINGTON BUNNY
SANCTUARY
Fluffy creatures welcome

"I declare this bunny sanctuary open!" said Lady Tottington as Gromit took a photo and a cage of bunnies in the Anti-pesto van broke into applause.

In a few minutes, Wallace and Gromit had set up the Bun-Vac and hundreds of happy bunnies were blown back into the ground.

"It's a dream come true, Wallace—my home, a safe haven for all things fluffy," sighed Lady Tottington.

"And a solution to all our storage problems!" said Wallace, watching the bunnies popping out of the ground all around Tottington Hall.

"I do hope you'll come and visit sometimes," said Lady Tottington. Wallace smiled.

"Oh, there'll always be a part of me here

at Tottington Hall . . ." replied Wallace.

Gromit pulled a lever and switched the Bun-Vac to full power.

"Really?" asked Lady Tottington.

"Oh, yes!" said Wallace, and with a huge pop, Hutch burst out of the Bun-Vac, struck a pose in mid-air, and bounced off across the lawn.